EVEN MORE
FARMYARD TALES

Heather Amery

Illustrated by Stephen Cartwright

Language Consultant: Betty Root

There is a little yellow duck to find on every page.

Notes for Parents

The stories in this delightful picture book are ones which your child will want to share with you many times.

All the stories in *Farmyard Tales* have been written in a special way to ensure that young children succeed in their first efforts to read.

To help with that success, first read the whole of one story aloud and talk about the pictures. Then encourage your child to read the short, simpler text at the top of each page and read the longer text at the bottom of the page yourself. This "turn about" reading builds up confidence and children do love joining in. It is a great day when they discover that they can read a whole story for themselves.

Farmyard Tales provides an enjoyable opportunity for parents and children to share the excitement of learning to read.

Betty Root

THE SILLY SHEEPDOG

This is Apple Tree Farm.

This is Mrs. Boot, the farmer. She has two children, called Poppy and Sam, and a dog called Rusty.

2

Ted works on Apple Tree Farm.

He has just bought a sheepdog to help him with the sheep. The sheepdog is called Patch.

Poppy, Sam and Rusty say hello to Patch.

"Come on, Patch," says Sam. "We'll show you all the animals on our farm."

4

First they look at the hens.

Patch jumps into the hen run and chases the hens.
They are frightened and fly up onto their house.

"Now we'll go and see the cows."

Patch runs into the field and barks at the cows.
But they just stand and stare at him.

6

Then they look at the pigs.

Patch jumps into the pig pen and chases all the pigs into their little house.

Sam shouts at Patch.

"Come here, you silly thing. You're meant to be a sheepdog. Ted will have to send you back."

8

They go to the sheep field.

"Look," says Sam. "One sheep is missing." "Yes, it's that naughty Woolly again," says Ted.

"Where's Patch going?" says Sam.

Patch runs away across the field. Ted, Sam, Poppy and Rusty run after him.

Patch dives through the hedge.

Patch barks and barks. "What has he found?"
says Sam. They all go to look.

Patch has found a boy.

The boy pats Patch. "Hello," he says. "I wondered who bought you when my Dad sold his farm."

The boy has found a sheep.

"There's Woolly," says Sam. "I found her on the road," says the boy . "I was bringing her back."

The boy whistles to Patch.

Patch chases Woolly back through the gate. She runs into the field with the other sheep.

Ted stares in surprise.

"Patch doesn't do anything I tell him," says Ted.
"You don't know how to whistle," says the boy.

15

Patch runs back to them.

"You must teach me how to whistle to Patch,"
says Ted. "He's not a silly dog after all," says Sam.

16

KITTEN'S DAY OUT

This is Apple Tree Farm.

This is Mrs. Boot, the farmer. She has two children called Poppy and Sam, and a dog called Rusty.

18

Ted works on the farm.

He is helping Mr. Bran, the truck driver. Mr. Bran has brought some sacks of food for the cows.

They say goodbye to Mr. Bran.

Mr. Bran waves as he drives his truck out of the yard. Ted and Poppy wave back.

20

"Where's my kitten?"

"Where's Fluff?" says Sam. They all look everywhere for Fluff. But they can't find her.

"Perhaps she jumped on the truck."

"Take my car and go after the truck, Ted," says Mrs. Boot. They jump in the car and drive off.

22

Ted stops the car at the crossroads.

"Which way did Mr. Bran go?" says Ted. "There's a truck," says Sam. "It's just going around the bend."

Ted drives down a steep hill.

"Look out Ted," says Poppy. There's a stream at the bottom. The car makes a big splash of water.

The car stops in the stream.

"Water in the engine," says Ted. "I'll have to push."
"We'll never find the truck now," says Sam.

Ted looks inside the car.

He mops up all the water. Soon he gets the car
to start again. They drive on to look for the truck.

There are lots of sheep on the road.

"The sheep came out of the field. Someone left the gate open," says Ted. "We must get them back."

Ted, Poppy and Sam round up the sheep.

They drive them back into the field. Ted shuts the gate. "Come on, we must hurry," says Sam.

28

"Stop, Ted, there's a truck."

"I'm sure that's Mr. Bran's truck in that farmyard," says Sam. Ted drives into the yard.

"It's the wrong truck."

"Oh dear," says Poppy. "It's not Mr. Bran and that's not Mr. Bran's truck."

Ted drives them home

"We'll never find my kitten now," says Sam.
"I'm sure she'll turn up," says Poppy.

There's a surprise at Apple Tree Farm.

"Here's your kitten," says Mr. Bran. "She's been in my truck all day and now I've brought her home."

THE NEW PONY

This is Apple Tree Farm.

This is Mrs. Boot, the farmer. She has two children, called Poppy and Sam, and a dog called Rusty.

34

Mr. Boot, Poppy and Sam go for a walk.

They see a new pony. "She belongs to Mr. Stone, who's just bought Old Gate Farm," says Dad.

The pony looks sad.

Her coat is rough and dirty. She looks hungry.
It looks as though no one takes care of her.

Poppy tries to stroke the pony.

"She's not very friendly," says Sam. "Mr. Stone says she's bad tempered," says Mr. Boot.

Poppy feeds the pony.

Every day, Poppy takes her apples and carrots.
But she always stays on the other side of the gate.

One day, Poppy takes Sam with her.

They cannot see the pony anywhere. The field looks empty. "Where is she?" says Sam.

Poppy and Sam open the gate.

Rusty runs into the field. Poppy and Sam are a bit scared. "We must find the pony," says Poppy.

"There she is," says Sam.

The pony has caught her head collar in the fence.
She has been eating the grass on the other side.

41

Poppy and Sam run home to Mr. Boot.

"Please come and help us, Dad," says Poppy. "The pony is caught in the fence. She will hurt herself."

Mr. Boot walks up to the pony.

He unhooks the pony's head collar from the fence.
"She's not hurt," says Dad.

"The pony's chasing us."

"Quick, run," says Sam. "It's all right," says Poppy,
patting the pony. "She just wants to be friends."

44

They see an angry man. It is Mr. Stone.

"Leave my pony alone," says Mr. Stone. "And get out of my field." He waves his stick at Poppy.

The pony is afraid of Mr. Stone.

Mr. Stone tries to hit the pony with his stick. "I'm going to get rid of that nasty animal," he says.

46

Poppy grabs his arm.

"You mustn't hit the pony," she cries. "Come on Poppy," says Mr. Boot. "Let's go home."

47

Next day, there's a surprise for Poppy.

The pony is at Apple Tree Farm. "We've bought her for you," says Mrs. Boot. "Thank you," says Poppy.

THE GRUMPY GOAT

This is Apple Tree Farm.

This is Mrs. Boot, the farmer. She has two children called Poppy and Sam, and a dog called Rusty.

Ted works on the farm.

He tells Poppy and Sam to clean the goat's shed.
"Will she let us?" asks Sam. "She's so grumpy now."

Gertie the goat chases Sam.

She butts him with her head. He nearly falls over.
Sam, Poppy and Rusty run out through the gate.

Poppy shuts the gate.

They must get Gertie out of her pen so they can get to her shed. "I have an idea," says Sam.

Sam gets a bag of bread.

"Come on, Gertie," says Sam. "Nice bread." Gertie
eats it and the bag but stays in her pen.

"Let's try some fresh grass," says Poppy.

Poppy pulls up some grass and drops it by the gate. Gertie eats it but trots back into her pen.

"I have another idea," says Sam.

"Gertie doesn't butt Ted. She wouldn't butt me if I looked like Ted," says Sam. He runs off again.

Sam comes back wearing Ted's clothes.

He has found Ted's old coat and hat. Sam goes
into the pen but Gertie still butts him.

"I'll get a rope," says Poppy.

They go into the pen. Poppy tries to throw the rope over Gertie's head. She misses.

Gertie chases them all.

Rusty runs out of the pen and Gertie follows him.
"She's out!" shouts Sam. "Quick, shut the gate."

Sam and Poppy clean out Gertie's shed.

They sweep up the old straw and put it in the wheelbarrow. They spread out fresh straw.

60

Poppy opens the gate.

"Come on, Gertie. You can go back now," says
Sam. Gertie trots back into her pen.

"You are a grumpy old goat," says Poppy.

"We've cleaned out your shed and you're still grumpy," says Sam. "Grumpy Gertie."

Next morning, they meet Ted.

"Come and look at Gertie now," says Ted. They all go to the goat pen.

Gertie has a little kid.

"Oh, isn't it sweet," says Poppy. "Gertie doesn't look grumpy now," says Sam.

First published in 1992. Usborne Publishing Ltd., Usborne House, 83-85 Saffron Hill, London EC1N 8RT, England. Copyright © Usborne Publishing Ltd., 1995, 1992